A Note to Parents and Caregivers:

Read-it! Readers are for children who are just starting on the amazing road to reading. These beautiful books support both the acquisition of reading skills and the love of books.

The RED LEVEL presents familiar topics using common words and repeating sentence patterns.

The BLUE LEVEL presents new ideas using a larger vocabulary and varied sentence structure.

The YELLOW LEVEL presents more challenging ideas, a broad vocabulary, and wide variety in sentence structure.

The GREEN LEVEL presents more complex ideas, an extended vocabulary range, and expanded language structures.

When sharing a book with your child, read in short stretches, pausing often to talk about the pictures. Have your child turn the pages and point to the pictures and familiar words. And be sure to reread favorite stories or parts of stories.

There is no right or wrong way to share books with children. Find time to read with your child, and pass on the legacy of literacy.

Adria F. Klein, Ph.D.
Professor Emeritus
California State University
San Bernardino, California

Editor: Bob Temple
Creative Director: Terri Foley
Editorial Adviser: Andrea Cascardi
Copy Editor: Laurie Kahn
Designer: Melissa Voda
Page production: The Design Lab
The illustrations in this book were painted with gouache.

Picture Window Books
5115 Excelsior Boulevard
Suite 232
Minneapolis, MN 55416
1-877-845-8392
www.picturewindowbooks.com

Printed in the United States of America.

Library of Congress Cataloging-in-Publication Data
White, Mark.
The lion and the mouse : a retelling of Aesop's fable / written by Mark White ;
illustrated by Sara Rojo.
p. cm. — (Read-it! Readers Fables)
Summary: A mouse begs a lion for mercy and, after he is set free, promises that
he will help the lion some day in return.
ISBN 1-4048-0216-9
[1. Folklore. 2. Fables.] I. Rojo, Sara, ill. II. Aesop. III. Title. IV. Series.
PZ8.2.W55 Li 2004
398.24'529757—dc21   2003006299

PICTURE WINDOW BOOKS

The Lion and the Mouse
A Retelling of Aesop's Fable

Written by Mark White

Illustrated by Sara Rojo

Library Adviser:
Kathy Baxter, M.A.
Former Coordinator of Children's Services
Anoka County (Minnesota) Library

Reading Advisers:
Adria F. Klein, Ph.D.
Professor Emeritus, California State University
San Bernardino, California

Susan Kesselring, M.A.
Literacy Educator
Rosemount-Apple Valley-Eagan (Minnesota) School District

Picture Window Books
Minneapolis, Minnesota

One afternoon, a tiny mouse
woke up from a nap.
He left his house
in search of a snack.

The little mouse closed
his eyes and sniffed.
How good the world smelled!

When he opened his eyes again,
he found himself in front
of the snout of an enormous
snoring lion!

6

7

The mouse tried to sneak away,
but his tiny shadow crossed
the lion's face. The lion woke up
and gave a tremendous yawn.

How scary all those teeth were!

A A A A W NNN!

"It looks like I've been awakened by a snack," the lion said.

He trapped the mouse's tail
under his large paw.

"Have mercy," begged the mouse.
"You are king of the forest,
and I am just a humble
little creature."

"You are right," said the lion.
"I am king of the forest.
And since you have found me
in a good mood,
I give you your freedom."

"Oh, thank you, Your Majesty," the mouse replied.
"And if one day you need my help, I will offer it with all my heart."

HAHA
HA

14

The lion began to laugh.
"How can such a tiny creature
help me? Can you help me to hunt?"

"No," answered the mouse.

"Don't worry, little one. You have
your freedom. You owe me nothing."

The lion disappeared into the forest,
but the mouse still could hear
his laughter.

15

The mouse soon smelled a delicious fruit and went back to his search for a snack.

This time, the mouse kept his eyes open while he followed his nose.

Then he heard a strange noise.

The mouse went back along the path he had followed. He found the lion trapped in a net.

"I'll help you!" shouted the mouse. The lion barely could hear the mouse's tiny shouts.

"What can you do, little one?" asked the lion. "It is better for you to run away, before the hunters return and catch you, too!"

The mouse stayed. He climbed up
into the tree and chewed at the net.

His teeth were not as large as the lion's,
but they were very sharp.

21

In a short while, the lion leaped
from the net. Free at last!

"You were right, my small friend,"
said the lion humbly. "You were able
to help me in my moment of need.
I owe you my life."

"Don't worry, Your Majesty," said the mouse.
"You have your freedom.
You owe me nothing."

The king of the forest and his new friend
disappeared into the trees together.

"You didn't think I could help you,"
the mouse said, "but an act of kindness
is never wasted."